Dear mouse friends,
Welcome to the world of

Geronimo Stilton

THE RODENT'S GAZETTE
EDITORIAL STAFF

Geronimo Stilton
A learned and brainy
mouse; editor of
The Rodent's Gazette

Thea Stilton
Geronimo's sister and
special correspondent at
The Rodent's Gazette

Trap Stilton
An awful joker;
Geronimo's cousin and
owner of the store
Cheap Junk for Less

Benjamin Stilton
A sweet and loving
nine-year-old mouse;
Geronimo's favorite
nephew

Geronimo Stilton

SINGING SENSATION

Scholastic Inc.

New York   Toronto   London   Auckland

Sydney   Mexico City   New Delhi   Hong Kong

No part of this publication may be reproduced, stored in a retrieval system, or transmitted in any form or by any means, electronic, mechanical, photocopying, recording, or otherwise, without written permission from the copyright holder. For information regarding permission, please contact: Atlantyca S.p.A., Via Leopardi 8, 20123 Milan, Italy; e-mail foreignrights@atlantyca.it, www.atlantyca.com.

ISBN 978-0-545-10368-8

Copyright © 2007 by Edizioni Piemme S.p.A., Via Tiziano 32, 20145 Milan, Italy.

International Rights © Atlantyca S.p.A.

English translation © 2009 by Atlantyca S.p.A.

GERONIMO STILTON names, characters, and related indicia are copyright, trademark, and exclusive license of Atlantyca S.p.A. All rights reserved. The moral right of the author has been asserted.

Based on an original idea by Elisabetta Dami.

www.geronimostilton.com

Published by Scholastic Inc., 557 Broadway, New York, NY 10012. SCHOLASTIC and associated logos are trademarks and/or registered trademarks of Scholastic Inc.

Stilton is the name of a famous English cheese. It is a registered trademark of the Stilton Cheese Makers' Association. For more information, go to www.stiltoncheese.com

Text by Geronimo Stilton
Original title *Lo strano caso del Sorcio Stonato*
Cover by Giuseppe Ferrario
Illustrations by Larry Keys Chiavini, Chiara Sacchi, Valentina Grassini, Flavio Ferron, and Valeria Brambilla
Graphics by Zeppola Zap, Michela Battaglin, and Brigitte Torri Vaccá

Special thanks to Kathryn Cristaldi
Translated by Lidia Morson Tramontozzi
Interior design by Kay Petronio

20 19 18 17 16 15 14 13   12 13 14 15 16/0

Printed in the U.S.A.   40
First printing, October 2009

THE FABUMOUSE MOZART!

It was a cold, rainy January night.

Lucky for me, I was warm and cozy inside my mouse hole. I was *nestled* in my favorite pawchair in front of a cheery fire.

"This is the life!" I squeaked, popping a **chocolate** cheese cupcake into my mouth and opening my book. I felt so relaxed. Everything was so peaceful. But then . . .

Rattle! Rattle!

The wind was rattling the windowpane right behind my chair!

I decided to play some soothing music.

Then I remembered I didn't have any music. My cousin Trap had borrowed all of my CDs for his cruise to the **Hamster Islands**.

That did it! I ran to my favorite music store. When I arrived, I waved hello to the shop owner, *Wild Willy Whistlewhiskers*. I made a mouseline straight for the *Classical Music* Department. I flipped through Beethoven, Bach, and Chopin until, at last, I found what I was looking for: Mozart. Have

you ever listened to Mozart? His music is FABUMOUSE!

The CD I wanted was in a rack next to a cello.

I walked around the cello and almost slipped on a banana peel.

Yikes! Who would leave a **banana** peel on the floor in a music store?

I began to flip through the CDs when someone stepped on my paw.

I looked around. **No one** was there.

I went back to the CDs.

Just then, someone pulled my fur.

I **WHIRLED** around. Again, there was no one in sight. Who was bothering me? I'm a nice mouse. I never do anything wrong. Well, except for that one time when I gave an old lady a stick of gum. How was I supposed to know she had dentures? The gum ripped those fake teeth right out of her mouth!

I was thinking about teeth when someone yanked my tail.

"**Yooo-hoo!**" a familiar voice called out.

A gray mouse wearing a long trench coat popped out from behind the cello.

It was my old friend, the famouse detective HeRcuLe PoiRat. Hercule loves to play pranks.

"Did you like my little joke, Geronimo?" Hercule giggled.

Then he got serious. "I need your help," he said. "You see, I found some stolen CDs and —"

"Sorry, got to run!" I squeaked, cutting off my friend. I love Hercule, but he always gets me involved in the *craziest* cases, and I had *too much work* to do.

I paid for my CD and **RACED OUT THE DOOR**. Hercule called after me, but I wasn't listening. The only rodent I wanted to listen to tonight was the fabumouse Mozart!

I wasn't listening!

MOUSE ISLAND IDOL

The next day, I got up early, gobbled down three large cheese doughnuts, and scampered to the office.

I had SO MUCH work to do. I had contracts to *sign*, articles to read, and bills to pay. Plus, I had to read through the entire edition of *The Rodent's Gazette* before it was printed. Just thinking about ALL of the work I had to do made my head spin. Oh, why was I always so stressed out? I felt a full-blown panic attack about to hit me.

Then the phone **rang**.

I jumped so high, my head left a dent in the ceiling. Well, OK, maybe not a *real* dent, but you get the picture.

"Hello, this is Stilton, *Geronimo Stilton*!" I squeaked into the phone.

"**Hey, Mr. G!**" a familiar rodent yelled. "What's happening? Are you still lifting those weights? Have you cut down on the disgusting doughnuts?"

I gulped, patting my tummy.

There is only one rodent I know who loves exercise more than cheese doughnuts. It was my super-fit, super-healthy, super-energetic friend **CHAMP STRONGPAWS**. Champ loves all kinds of endurance sports like cycling, swimming, and running. But most of all he **loves** marathons. Not too long ago he even signed me up to run in the Mouse Island Marathon. On

race day, I was so scared, I almost passed out before I even reached the starting line! Did I mention I'm not much of a *sportsmouse*? In fact, my sister, Thea, likes to say I have four left paws.

"Hi, Champ," I squeaked **NERVOUSLY.** I prayed he hadn't signed me up for another **crazy** race.

But Champ didn't call to talk about marathons. It was worse. Much worse.

"You take showers, right, Mr. G?" Champ asked. "Of course I do!" I replied indignantly. I took pride in being a well-dressed, clean-smelling, very **NEAT** rodent.

"And you sing in the shower, don't you?" he asked. I felt my cheeks heat up. How did Champ know I sang in the shower? How **embarrassing**!

"How do you know that?" I asked.

"Well, Mr. G, I was walking by your house the other day and I heard you singing in the **SHOWER**. That's when I came up with a great **IDEA**! I'm signing you up to be on

YOU'VE GOT
TO BE JOKING!

My fur stood on end. Have you ever seen *Mouse Island Idol*? It is a TV show where mice with amazing singing voices compete to become Mouse Island's best squeaker.

"You've got to be *joking*!" I shrieked into the phone. "I can't sing on TV!"

"I'm telling you, Mr. G, you've got real talent," Champ insisted. "Now here's what I need you to do. Start **gargling** with warm water to get your vocal cords going, do three hundred jumping jacks to get your blood pumping, and **I'll be right over**."

My jaw hit the ground. "What?!" I protested. "We can't get together now! I've got a ton of work to do."

CHAMP STRONGPAWS

First Name: Champ

Last Name: Strongpaws

Background info: An all-around star athlete. He's into the latest training trends. He works for a sports radio station, and loves to get lazy rodents up and running.

Sports: He does all kinds of endurance sports like cycling, running, and swimming. And he loves marathons!

His advice: Eat right, sleep right, and keep those paws pumping!

What he believes in: Exercise!

His passion: Exploring new countries and getting to experience other cultures.

His slogan: "Sports can make the world a better place!"

His claim to fame: He built a super-fast bicycle that can seat five mice!

His dream: To explore the ten most beautiful countries in the world in ten days, with ten different bicycles.

A loud buzzing sound interrupted me.

It was coming from the phone. Yes, my crazy friend had hung up on me!

Two minutes later, I glanced out of the window. Alarmed, I saw a **bizarre** rodent arriving at warp speed on a bicycle. He was wearing a helmet, a yellow cyclist suit, and mirrored sunglasses. His head was bent so low, he looked like he was trying to eat the handlebars. He disappeared into the building, still on his bike. A second later, my door flew open. Champ **ZOOMED** into the room and skidded to a spectacular stop in front of my desk. He didn't dismount. Instead, he grabbed my paw and squeezed it so hard, I thought I would faint.

"*Soooooooooooooo great to see you, Mr. G!*" he exclaimed.

ARE YOU EXCITED?

While I checked my paw for broken bones, Champ started squeaking.

"So, are you excited about the TV show?" he asked with a chuckle. "Are your whiskers SHIVERING with anticipation? Don't stress a bit! We'll have the public eating out of our paws!"

The door flew open again, and Pinky Pick, my editorial assistant, scampered in.

"HEY, BOSS MOUSE!" she shrieked. "You didn't tell me you were going to be on TV! Who knew you could sing? You can barely whistle!"

I felt a GIANT, mouse-size HEADACHE coming on. "I am

not going to be on TV!" I started to squeak.

Just then, I heard a thump outside my door. I raced to open it and was hit with an **avalanche** of rodents. Cheese niblets! My entire staff was eavesdropping on me!

They all started squeaking at once.

"Mr. Stilton's going to be famouse!"

"Our boss, the next Mouse Island Idol!"

My whiskers whirled with **frustration**. How did I get myself into these situations? Finally, I couldn't take it anymore.

"**ENOUGH!**" I cried. "I am not going to be famouse! I am not going to be on TV!"

Dead silence fell on the entire place.

It was then that my little nephew Benjamin came in. He hugged me **HAPPILY**.

"Uncle Geronimo, are you really going to be on the show?" he asked. "I've always dreamed of going to see *Mouse Island Idol.* **Uncle Geronimo**, I'm so proud of you! May I come with you?"

My heart melted. What could I do? I can never say no to my dear nephew. He means the world to me.

"Yes, Benjamin. I'll go on the show," I agreed. "And you can **CHEER** me on!"

It's great to love one another! It's great to love one another! It's great to love one another! It's great to love one another!

WHY DO I HAVE TO TAKE A COLD SHOWER?

The following morning, I was dreaming happily of warm cheddar melts and sandy beaches when the doorbell **rang**.

I sat bolt upright. According to my clock, it was five in the morning. Who would ring my doorbell at this **unmousely** time of the morning? Was there a fire down at *The Rodent's Gazette*? Had my sister, Thea, crashed her motorcycle?

I scampered to the front door, my whiskers twitching **NERVOUSLY**.

But when I yanked open the door, all I saw was Champ perched on a bicycle.

"Wake up, Mr. G!" he squeaked in my

snout. "Today is your first day of training. From now on, you will wake up at **five** A.M., take a **COLD SHOWER**, and then head to voice lessons. At **six** A.M., you'll take a **COLD SHOWER**, then head to ballet lessons. At **seven** A.M., you'll take a **COLD SHOWER**, then head to ballroom dancing. At **eight** A.M, you'll take a **COLD SHOWER**, then head to piano lessons. At **nine** A.M., you'll take a **COLD SHOWER**, then —"

My head was spinning. I held up my paw to interrupt him. "Why do I have to take a **COLD SHOWER**?" I interrupted.

With a smile, Champ showered me with a bucket of **icy, cold** water.

I let out a whisker-curling yell.

"**Aaaaaaaaaaaaaaaaaaaaaaahhhhhh!**"

Champ's smile widened.

"See how well you can scream? That's how

you make those vocal cords stronger! No need to thank me, Mr. G," Champ explained.

Thank him? I was so mad I could have strangled him with my bare paws. I chased after Champ, screaming my head off, **"If I catch you ..."**

"That's it, Mr. G!" Champ cheered. **"Keep screaming!"**

Oh, how did I get myself into this mess?

PERFORMING ARTS SCHOOL

Champ took me to the **MOUSE ISLAND SCHOOL OF PERFORMING ARTS**. The students there were so talented. Plus, the classes were **REALLY HARD**. I wanted to quit. But then I remembered the promise I had made to my nephew Benjamin. I couldn't disappoint him.

So, for three whole months, I stuck to Champ's crazy schedule. I had some **amazing** teachers at school. They taught me to read music, to play an instrument, and to sing and **dance**.

It was exhausting, but I have to admit, it was also kind of fun.

Now if only I could get used to those **COLD SHOWERS**!

1. Singing Lessons:

The voice teacher taught me how to sing outside the shower.

2. Ballet Lessons:

The ballet teacher taught me how to dance on tippy paws.

3. Ballroom Dancing Lessons:

The ballroom dancing teacher taught me how to dance the tango.

4. Piano Lessons:

The piano teacher didn't yell when I got my paws mixed up.

5. Music History Lessons:

The history teacher taught me about Beethoven and Tchaikovsky.

6. Modern Music Lessons:

Champ took me to a radio station where we got to be deejays for a day!

SQUEAK IT UP!

ONE DAY AFTER MY LESSONS, Champ picked me up at the performing arts school.

"You're in for a big surprise, Mr. G!" he announced.

I gulped. Champ's surprises were usually my **NIGHTMARES**.

Champ drove like a wild mouse through the busy streets of New Mouse City. Along

the way, we nearly mowed down a mouse selling **hot** cheesy pretzels, a delivery rodent, and a mother mouse pushing her baby mouseling in a stroller.

"Watch it!" they all cried.

By the time we got to our destination, my fur was standing on end. Champ dragged me into an ENORMOUSE SKYSCRAPER. We got into an elevator with mirrored walls. Champ pushed a button, and we shot like a missile to the thirty-sixth floor.

"Welcome to Mousey Records," the receptionist greeted us. *Holey cheese! I thought. Mousey Records is the most popular record label in New Mouse City!*

We followed the receptionist down a **long**, carpeted hallway into a *luxurious* glass office. A serious-looking bunch of rodents stared at us from behind a huge table.

"So you're the new talent Champ has been telling us about," one of the mice said.

"**Sing something**," another instructed.

"Yeah, squeak it up," a third agreed.

I was so nervous, I thought I might **faint**. My teeth began chattering. My paws trembled. Everyone stared at me, waiting.

"Well, um, I . . ." I stammered.

Just then, a terrible pain shot up my spine. I let out a screech.

I looked down. Champ was standing on my tail.

The record executives didn't seem to notice.

"Amazing!" they gushed. "You were right, Champ. We'll have him record a CD and we'll send it to *Mouse Island Idol*."

The biggest mouse picked up the phone.

"I'll ask the president of **Mousey Records** if he agrees."

He spoke on the phone for a few seconds, then hung up the receiver looking very pleased.

"The president said he heard that **YELL** all the way up on the forty-sixth floor! It's a go!"

I could hardly believe it. It felt like one minute I was singing in the shower, and the next I was cutting a CD for Mousey Records!

6

In the recording studio, lots of rodents work together to make the record a success:

THE PRESIDENT!

The director of marketing, who releases the record!

The lawyer, who deals with legal questions!

The publisher, who follows its production to the end!

8

The store owners, who sell the CDs!

7

The distributors, who make sure the CDs arrive in every store!

WELCOME TO NEW MOUSE CITY!

The record executives introduced me to a songwriter. He said he had just written a song that was **perfect** for me: "Welcome to New Mouse City." I felt so honored. I felt so special. I felt so . . . nervous! How could I, Geronimo Stilton, sing such an *important song*?

Champ shoved a guitar in my paws. I gulped. **Stars** appeared before my eyes. Then another picture popped into my head. It was of my dear nephew **Benjamin**. What could I do? I had to sing. So I did.

Welcome to New Mouse City

Welcome to New Mouse City,
where the streets are, oh, so pretty,
and the mice are so nice,
you'll come back at least twice
to the fabumouse New Mouse City!

If you're looking to eat,
you are in for a treat.
New Mouse City is known for its cheeses.
There are tasty buffets and cheddar cafés
and waterfront dining with breezes.

If you prefer to shop,
New Mouse City's your stop.
You can buy almost anything here:
tail combs, fancy ties, whisker curlers, and pies.
You can even get rock-climbing gear.

Yes, welcome to New Mouse City,
where the streets are, oh, so pretty,
and the mice are so nice,
you'll come back at least twice
to the fabumouse New Mouse City!

At night, the lights of the city shine bright.
All rodents are charmed by the magical sight.
You can take in a show or hit museum row.
New Mouse City's a treasure wherever you go.

Yes, welcome to New Mouse City,
where the streets are, oh, so pretty,
and the mice are so nice,
you'll come back at least twice
to the fabumouse New Mouse City!

A NEW LOOK

When I was done singing, everyone at **Mousey Records** cheered. But then, I noticed Champ and some of the record executives all huddled in a corner. They kept staring at me and whispering.

I started to get worried.

What was wrong? Was my singing too loud? Too soft? Too high? Too **LOW**? Or could it possibly be too . . . squeaky? Yes, I decided that must be it.

I hung my head. My tail drooped. Now Benjamin would never get to see me on TV.

BZZZZZZ . . . bzzz. . . . BZZZZZZ. . . .

Too squeaky, I thought, then sighed. I felt lower than a sewer rat. But then I started to feel annoyed. Of course my voice sounded squeaky. After all, I was a mouse, wasn't I? Mice are supposed to sound **squeaky**.

I marched up to Champ and his new pals. But before I could say a word, Champ pulled me aside.

"Mr. G, we've decided you need someone to help you with your *LOOK*," he said.

"And I have the perfect rodent."

At first, I was insulted. I mean, what was wrong with my *LOOK*? I take a shower every day. I BRUSH my fur. And I always floss after a big meal. Then I thought about my wardrobe. It wasn't exactly exciting.

"I guess it would be fun to have someone help me pick out some new clothes," I agreed. "He's an **expert**, right?" At

this, Champ gave me a **sly look**.

"*She's* an **expert**," he grinned.

"She?" I asked. "It's a female mouse?"

Champ gave me another look.

"Yes, she's a **very young** young female mouse," he said. "In fact, you know her well. She works for you."

Suddenly, I had a terrible feeling in the pit of my stomach.

WHY, WHY, WHY DID I LET MYSELF BE DRAGGED INTO SUCH A MESS?

There is only one **veRy younG** female mouse at *The Rodent's Gazette*.

"Not **Pinky Pick**!" I screeched. Pinky is my extremely brainy but extremely annoying editorial assistant.

"She's the one!" Champ squeaked as he jumped on his bike and raced for the door.

I tried to run after him, but he was too *FAST*.

Over the next several days, Pinky got me to try out different 𝓛☺☺𝓚𝓢.

EACH ONE LOOKED CRAZIER THAN THE NEXT.

RAP

REGGAE

PUNK

But, in the end, I decided to stick with **my own look** and just be myself.

No More Cheesy
Chews for You!

The next day, I was sitting in my office munching on a **yummy** chocolate cheese doughnut when my door flew open. Can you guess who it was? Yes, it was Champ.

He ran up to me and **ripped** the doughnut out of my paw.

"What do you think you're doing, Mr. G?" he squeaked. "You can't be eating junk like this if you want to make it on *Mouse Island Idol*! You need to start eating right!"

"But . . . but . . . but . . ." I stammered. Champ interrupted me.

"No 'buts,' Mr. G," he ordered. "From now on, I'm putting you on a **STRICT DIET**. You will

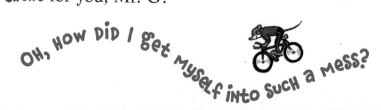

eat only HEALTHY FOODS like fruits, vegetables, and whole grains."

He plunked a big basket filled with nutritious foods on my desk.

Then I listened halfheartedly as Champ read off a list of foods I couldn't eat.

"No candy, no cakes, no cookies, no fried foods . . ."

His voice droned on and on. I kept thinking of the delicious box of Cheesy Chews I had at home in my fridge. Good thing I hadn't brought it to work. Champ would have tossed it with my doughnut!

"Oh, and one more thing," Champ added before he raced out the door. "I climbed through the window of your mouse hole and cleaned out your whole place. No more Cheesy Chews for you, Mr. G!"

Oh, how did I get myself into such a mess?

BUT WHAT ABOUT THE TRAIN?

A week later, my doorbell rang at four A.M.

Ding-dong! Ding-dong! Ding-dong!

I dragged myself out of bed. Who was waking me up so early? I yanked open my door and almost got run over by Champ on his bicycle. I should have known.

"This is it, Mr. G," Champ announced. "Tonight is the big night. You are scheduled to appear on *Mouse Island Idol*!"

My **PAWS** started to tremble. My fur stood on end. "Tonight?!" I shrieked. "But I'm not ready!" I was a nervous wreck!

Champ clapped me on the back.

"Of course you're ready, Mr. G," he said confidently. "All you need to do is warm up your voice, and you're good to go! *Just pack up your suit, change into these bike shorts, and we're off!"*

Bike shorts?

The TV studio where they filmed **Mouse Island Idol** was all the way in Mousefort Beach. That was more than **150 miles** away! I'd never make it there on a bike.

"But what about the train?" I protested.

Champ rolled his eyes. "Let's go, Mr. G," he said, rolling over my paw and out the door.

Oh, how did I get myself into this mess?

* Mouse
Island
Idol *

New Mouse City

MOUSEFORT BEACH

A QUICK RATNAP

By the time we arrived, I was so tired, I could barely keep my **EYES** open. Champ, on the other paw, was full of energy. He zipped off to register me.

I was relieved. Now was my chance to catch a quick **ratnap**. I curled up on the sidewalk and fell asleep. I dreamed I was riding my bike through the Mousehara Desert. It was boiling **HOT**. Suddenly, I spotted a lake in the distance. I pedaled toward the lake, but my bike hit a rock. I went flying over the handlebars and landed in a pile of **MOUSETRAPS**. **YOUUUUUUUCH!** I screamed so loud, I woke myself up.

Champ was standing over me. No, he was standing *on* me. On my **PAW**, to be exact!

"Nice squeaking, Mr. G!" he smirked.

But there was no time to get **UPSET**. I was about to sing on national TV! Champ said there were four other contestants before me. Each would sing a song, and then he or she would be judged by a panel of *celebrity* rodents.

Just thinking about being onstage made my whiskers tremble.

Oh, how did I get myself into such a mess? I wasn't a singer. I was about to grab my tail and run when I felt a tug on my paw.

I looked down. It was my **dear** nephew Benjamin. "Isn't this **EXCITING**, Uncle Geronimo?" he breathed. "I can't believe I'm going to watch my favorite uncle on my favorite TV show — *Mouse Island Idol!*"

DON'T THINK ABOUT IT!

I felt better knowing that Benjamin would be cheering me on. Still, I had **butterflies** in my stomach. And my paws were shaking so hard, I almost tripped on our way into the **studio**.

Get a grip, Geronimo, I coached myself. *All you have to do is sing one song. How* **BAD** *can you be? After all, you've been practicing every day for three months. And even if you're the worst squeaker, at least you'll show Benjamin you're not a quitter.*

We gathered backstage so that I could wait for my turn. I listened to the other singers. They were **good**, but I told myself that I was good, too. I started to feel **BETTER**.

Then Champ put his paw around me.

"Relax, Mr. G," he advised. "You'll be great. Don't think about the **HUNDREDS OF MILLIONS** of rodents watching you from **around the world**. Don't think about the **eggs** they'll hurl at you if you stink!"

I gulped.

"Don't think about tripping onstage. Don't think about **forgetting** the words to the song," Champ went on.

I shivered. By now, the gentle **butterflies** in my stomach had turned into an **angry mob**.

"And definitely don't think about getting a tongue cramp. **That would be the worst**," Champ continued.

I wanted to **scream**. I wanted to **cry**. I wanted to put a sock in Champ's snout. But he kept right on squeaking.

The more I tried not to think of things, the more I thought of them!

We entered the **THEATER** where the **festival** was being held. **CHAMP** grabbed me by the tail. I didn't even realize that he had pushed me. I only knew that all of a sudden I was on the stage of the festival.

I saw **Rattisio**, the most famous master of ceremonies on Mouse Island.

I was overwhelmed by emotion just to be here with him!

"Good evening, everyone!" he squeaked confidently. "Ladies and gentlemice, I give you a new artist who is participating in the *festival* for the first time! Geronimo Stilton, who will sing '**Welcome to New Mouse City**'!"

He winked an eye and whispered, "Cheer up, and *good luck*!"

He adjusted the microphone in front of my snout and disappeared!

I was the ONLY ONE ONSTAGE. NOW, it was MY turn.

Cheese niblets!

A CRAMPED TONGUE!

Holey cheese! The place was packed. The audience stared up at me expectantly.

The **STAGE LIGHTS** grew brighter. They were so bright, I couldn't see a thing!

I swallowed hard. For some reason, my tongue felt huge in my **mouth**. But I had to

sing. Everyone was waiting for me. I took a **deep breath** and opened my mouth, but nothing came out. Not even one little squeak.

Rat-munching rattlesnakes! Could this really be happening?

Could I really have gotten a cramp in my tongue?

No, it couldn't be. I took another breath and tried again. Still nothing came out. I was horrified.

"Squeak it up! Squeak it up!" the crowd began to chant.

I didn't know what to do. I was frozen with **FEAR**. Just when I thought I would faint, Benjamin appeared at my side.

"Don't be nervous, Uncle," he said. "I know you can do it. You just have to **believe** in yourself."

Then he began to sing in his sweet little mouseling voice.

I was so touched. Before I knew it, I was **SINGING** out loud and clear along with him.

All of the young mouselings in the audience joined in. Our song filled the studio. I'm not sure what the judges thought, but it sounded *fabumouse* to me!

la la la la la la la la la la la la la la la la la la

WHY ME?

When we finished singing, a hush fell over the audience.

I was worried.

Moldy mozzarella, did I sound that bad? I thought.

Then thunderous applause erupted.

The judges declared me the winner. I, Geronimo Stilton, was the new **Mouse Island Idol**! What an honor!

I invited my friends at **Mousey**

Records onstage. After all, I couldn't have done it without them.

Champp shook my paw.

"**GREAT JOB**, Mr. G!" he shouted. "I almost thought you believed my tongue-cramp story. But you knew I was **joking**, right? I mean, only a furbrain would believe you can get a cramp in your tongue," he chuckled.

I felt the **BLOOD** rushing to my face. Then I felt a searing pain as Champ rolled off with my tail caught in his bicycle spokes!

I let out a whisker-curling yell. "**SQUEAK!**"

The crowd went wild.

"What a voice!" they cheered.

It took three rolls of tape to bandage my tail.

"WHY, WHY, WHY DID I LET MYSELF BE DRAGGED INTO SUCH A MESS?"
I sobbed.

THAT'S STEALING!

In three weeks, I had become a singing sensation! "Welcome to New Mouse City" was put on a CD. Mice everywhere were listening to my song—in the subway, in the park, and even at the supermarket!

Then one day, Champ called. "Something **weird** is going on," he said. "Mousey Records says they've hardly sold any of your CDs. Someone must be pirating your record!"

I had no idea what Champ was talking about. Tons of rodents were playing my CD. Mousey Records had to be selling copies.

And what did **PIRATES** have to do with anything?

Champ explained what it meant to pirate a CD. First the thief buys a CD from a store. Then he makes a lot of copies, sells them, and keeps all the money.

"That's **STEALING**!" I cried.

There was only one thing to do.

"This is a case for **HERCULE POIRAT**!" I squeaked.

HERCULE POIRAT

A Total Rattrap!

I took off for Hercule's agency. Oh, excuse me. Do you remember **Hercule Poirat** from the beginning of this story? He is not only my friend; he is also the world's most famouse mouse detective!

Even though Hercule is famouse, his office is a complete disaster. It is located in a **RUndOWn** building sandwiched between two sleek skyscrapers. Hercule's office is **such a mess**, some clients refuse to meet him there. They will only do business over the phone. But Hercule doesn't care.

"I love my messy office," he always

says. "It reminds me of *my home sweet home*."

Hercule was right about that. His home was a total rattrap!

I knocked on the door.

KNOCK, KNOCK, KNOCK!

Just then, a sticky red liquid rained down on my head.

Was it **blood**?

I was about to faint when the door opened.

"Is that you, Geronimo?" Hercule giggled when he saw me. "What do you think of my new antiburglar device? Don't look so upset. It's just **ketchup**."

He gave me a towel and I did my best to wipe the sticky stuff off me. Oh, why had

I bothered to take a shower that morning? I felt worse than the time I accidentally fell into a vat of **macaroni and cheese** at the Cheese Place Factory. I was sticky then, too, but at least I was covered in yummy cheese!

I took two pawsteps into Hercule's office. What a **disaster**!

There was **JUNK** everywhere! Books, **CRUMPLED** papers, dirty dishes, and old **banana** peels covered the floor. I saw a patched-up old chair in one corner of the room and a piece of **moldy** pizza on the desk. It really was disgusting. But I didn't bother mentioning it to Hercule.

He was a slob and he was proud of it. Plus, I had more important things to discuss.

I told Hercule that my CD had been pirated. **"Will you help me?"** I asked.

??? A Crook in a Camper

Hercule stamped his paw, sending up a cloud of **dust**. "I told you **someone was stealing CDs**!" he squeaked. "Remember when I asked for your help on this case?"

Somewhere in the back of my brain, I did remember. I apologized to Hercule.

Then I asked, "What do we do now?"

"I've got it all under **CONTROL**, Geronimo," Hercule answered. "Come back tonight, and we'll sniff out this case together."

Later that evening, I scampered back to Hercule's office. I knocked on the door.

KNOCK, KNOCK, KNOCK!

A sack of flour bonked me on the head. I was covered from head to tail in white powder.

"WHY ME?!" I shrieked. Hercule appeared at the door. "How do you like the flour, Geronimo?" he asked. "I ran out of ketchup."

I dusted myself off. Then I went in.

"I was just making a **banana** shake," Hercule said, hitting a button on the blender. "Want some?"

I shook my head. I know they're healthy, but I can't stand bananas. When the drink was ready, Hercule slurped it down in one gulp. Then he let out a loud **burp**.

I made a mental note to return the magnifying glass

I had bought my friend for Christmas. I'd use the money to buy him a subscription to *Gentlemouse Weekly* instead!

I was still thinking about *Gentlemouse Weekly* when Hercule's phone rang.

"I've got **some exciting news**, Geronimo," Hercule announced after he hung up. "The police need me to track down a **mysterious black** camper. It belongs to **a thief** whose nickname is the **Musical Pirate**."

According to the police, the **Musical Pirate** was stealing CDs and making copies of them. Then he passed them off to a rat named **Sleezer**, who sold them to the innocent mice of New Mouse City.

Now I knew who had stolen my CD. But there was still one problem.

How do you catch a crook in a camper?

THE CRUELCAT
EXPRESS

I should have known Hercule already had a plan. That night at midnight, we scampered down to the waterfront. According to Hercule, the **Musical Pirate** was due to meet Sleezer's henchmice at **PIER 13**.

It was cold, dark, and spooky at the pier. To make matters worse, Hercule had insisted we

disguise ourselves as **fishermice**.

Before I could say "squeak!" he had sprayed me with a gallon of fish oil. *I stunk like a rotten fish market on a hot summer day.*

Hours went by with no action. Then, we heard a strange **SOUND**, like a cat hissing. *HISSSSSSS!*

The fur on my tail stood on edge, and my *whiskers* *trembled*. I saw a black camper with what appeared to be cat's ears on top.

Then I read the name under the front windshield: Cruelcat Express.

The camper was incredibly **long**, with no windows. What a **NIGHTMARE**!

Did I mention I'm afraid of windowless places?

The camper parked along the pier.

An invisible door opened with a swish. A cat whose fur was as dark as a MOONLESS NIGHT stepped out. He wore a **sleek** black raincoat with the initials **P.P.** on it, and steel-toed boots. His eyes were two slits of **icy blue**, and a long scar slashed his left cheek.

CatBerry

The strange electronic gadget **P.P.** always wears around his neck.

It can be used to make phone calls, send e-mails, play music, and activate an alarm.

Around his neck, he wore a strange electronic gadget. When he tapped it, I gasped. He had a $STEEL$ PAW!

I was thinking of how much he reminded me of a PIRATE when the headlights of the camper flickered. A trapdoor opened in the back, and cases of something began to roll out. It didn't take us long to realize they were filled with pirated CDs!

Sleezer's henchmice loaded the boxes into a van. So this was how my song had been stolen!

A BLISTER ON MY LEFT PAW

When the van was fully loaded, the crooked mice **TOOK OFF**. Only the black camper and the mysterious pirate remained. He stared out over the water. Then he unwrapped a piece of **black** gum and began chomping on it noisily. After a few minutes, he slipped back into the camper. But first, he spat the gum out and threw the wrapper into the ocean. What a littercat!

I WAS SO DISGUSTED.

"That's it," I told Hercule. "I've seen enough. Let's go home."

Of course, Hercule had other ideas.

"ARE YOU CRAZY, GERONIMO?!" he squeaked. "Now is our time to do some real **SPYING**.

I'll stand guard while you go check out the Cruelcat Express."

I tried to refuse. I mean, Hercule was the detective, right? Plus, it's no secret that I'm a bit of a scaredy mouse. Well, OK, I'm actually a BIG scaredy mouse, but no one has to know that.

Finally, I gave in.

"I'd go myself, but I have a blister on my left paw," Hercule said as he shoved me toward the camper.

His voice trailed off as I crept closer to the camper.

Oh, how did I get myself into this mess? It was Saturday night. I should have been home with a big bowl of cheddar popcorn, watching a movie.

Or maybe playing a game at my favorite bowling alley, **Lucky Paw Lanes**.

At that moment, the driver's door of the Cruelcat Express opened, and two muscular-looking cats came out.

I flattened myself against the side of the camper.

Luckily, the two thugs didn't even glance my way.

"That was a great idea the boss had to copy those CDs inside the camper, right, Ding-Dong?" one cat chuckled.

"You said it, Ding-a-Ling," the other guffawed. "Guess he'll be using the money to do more **WICKED THINGS** on Cat Island."

I gasped. Cat Island? Could there be a **SCARIER** place?

PEE PEE!

I crept back to Hercule.

"Those crooks are from Cat Island!" I **squeaked**.

My paws trembled as I dialed Champ on my cell phone. I had to tell him we had found the **Musical Pirate**.

But just as I was starting to explain about the Cruelcat Express, and the pirate with the steel paw, something terrible happened.

My cell phone was tossed into the water.

I wish I could say it slipped out of my paws, but it was worse. **Much worse.**

We had been discovered!

I stared helplessly into the icy cold eyes of the mysterious **Musical Pirate**.

"What do you think you **rodents** are doing?!" he growled. "How dare you **SPY** on the great, the cunning, and, might I add, the purrfectly handsome **Pussycat Pulverizer**, also known as **P.P.** for short?"

To my horror, at that moment, Hercule collapsed in a fit of **laughter**.

"Excuse me, did you say your name was Pee Pee?" he asked with a laugh.

"As in, where is the potty? I have to go Pee pee?"

Pussycat Pulverizer looked like he was about to explode. **STEAM** shot from his ears.

"They're my initials, **FOOL**!" he hissed.

Hercule just smirked. "Whatever you say, Pee Pee," he said.

P.P. appeared to be growing angrier by the minute. I had to do something.

"Um, **Mr. P.P.**, sir, we are just poor fishermice passing through," I said meekly as I tried to scoot away from him. "We'll get out of your fur now."

P.P. wrinkled his nose.

"You do **stink** like fish, but I say you're spies!" he roared.

He grabbed his **CatBerry**.

"BE READY TO LEAVE IN AN HOUR!" he yelled into the device.

Just then, a cat with white fur and a black spot around his eye began to **whine**.

"But, Cousin, we just got here," he mewed. "I wanted to get a mug of fresh milk and a plate of sardines at

CLEVELAND
(AKA P.P.'s LITTLE COUSIN)

the Ratsnest Diner. I heard they serve cats."

P.P. rolled his eyes.

"**Forget it, Cleveland**," he hissed.

Cleveland stamped his paws. "No fair! I **never** get to do anything fun!" he started to whine. Then he stopped.

P.P. was glaring at him with a **DEADLY** look in his eyes.

"Oops, did I say that? Sometimes my words get so m-m-m-mixed up," Cleveland stammered. "I always have fun when I'm around you, C-C-C-Cousin. Better get packing. Hey, maybe I can whip up a **black**

eel pie for dinner and some of that fancy **black licorice** you like so much."

As Cleveland slunk away, a tall cat with **STEEL-STUDDED** bracelets on each paw

PUSSYCAT PULVERIZER

Who is he? A mean, nasty cat who travels around in a long black camper called the Cruelcat Express.

Nickname: The Musical Pirate

What does he do? He makes copies of stolen CDs in his high-tech camper. He never stays in the same place, so it's difficult for the authorities to catch him.

Unusual markings: His right paw is made out of steel.

His battle cry: "We are ca-ca-cats and we eat ra-ra-rats!"

His plan: To sell thousands of pirated CDs so he can become rich, rich, rich!

His weakness: Black licorice chewing gum

His dream: To become the most powerful cat on Cat Island.

PUNY

strode over to us. His name was **PUNY**, but he was as big as my uncle Bigbelly's industrial-size **refrigerator**!

Puny took everything we had in our pockets.

Then he turned toward **P.P.**

"What should we do with these **good-for-nothing** rodents, Boss?" he asked.

A few minutes later, Hercule and I found ourselves tied up in a room with lots of recording equipment.

"This place has soundproof walls, so don't even bother **SCREAMING**," Puny advised before he left.

Oh, how did I get myself into **SUCH a mess**?

GARLIC MOUSE ROAST

"Putrid cheese puffs!" Hercule complained.
"I wish they hadn't emptied our pockets. I
had some of my best gadgets
with me. Like my super-duper
cheese slicer and pocketknife.
And my ultra-cool laser-beam
ballpoint pen. And
my compact pawnail

**super-duper
cheese slicer and
pocketknife**

**ultra-cool
laser-beam
ballpoint pen**

**compact
pawnail filer**

filer. This stinks! What if I get a
HANGNAIL?"

For a while, we both stared into
space, not saying a word. I think
we were both too **down in the
dumps** to squeak.

Then Hercule started to giggle

uncontrollably. At first, I was alarmed. Was he having a medical **EMERGENCY**? Did he need a psychiatrist? Was he that worried about his missing pawnail filer?

Fortunately, it was none of those things. Hercule had just come up with a brilliant escape plan.

It started with him yelling his favorite battle cry, "Have NO fear, Hercule Poirat is here!"

Next he gnawed at our ropes like a starving rat.

In a few minutes, we were **free**!

Hercule hid behind the door. Then I yelled through the door.

"Excuse me, Mr. **PUNY**," I called. "Can you come here for a minute?"

I heard some shuffling outside the door.

"Oh, why'd you wake me up?" **PUNY** grumbled. "I was dreaming I was eating a

juicy garlic mouse roast. It was *so tasty*."

PUNY pulled open the door, and as he did, Hercule clobbered him on the head with a **HEAVY** speaker.

The humongous cat went down like a ton of hard cheese.

BLACK VELVET
WALLPAPER

"Let's go!" Hercule whispered.

We tiptoed around **PUNY** and found ourselves in a long hallway covered with `black` velvet wallpaper. My teeth chattered. What a dark and **SPOOKY** place!

I shivered. We were in **P.P.**'s private apartment!

I was so **SCARED**, I felt like I could jump out of my own fur. I tried not to scream as we passed an aquarium filled with **piranhas**.

Then something caught my eye that made my heart stop. A cat in a black raincoat sat hunched over a computer screen. Yep, it was **Pussycat Pulverizer** himself! He was staring at a string of numbers that were **flashing** across the monitor.

"I'm rich, rich, **RICH**!" he meowed. "I've made more money selling these pirated CDs than I've made in my whole nine lives!"

He picked up his **CatBerry**, chuckling wickedly.

"We leave for Cat Island in an hour!" he announced. "Get packing!"

I was ready to pack it up myself when the **worst** thing happened.

P.P. turned and spotted us.

"**Catch them!**" he shrieked.

Just then, I heard a familiar voice shouting outside.

"Give yourselves up!" the voice bellowed. "You're surrounded!"

It was **CHaMP StRoNgPawS**!

With a cry, **P.P.** began shrieking into his **CatBerry**, "Attention, all felines on the **CRUELCAT EXPRESS**! This is an **EMERGENCY**! I repeat, **EMERGENCY**! Everyone to the submarine! **Now**!"

A MYSTERIOUS
SUBMARINE

There was no time to waste. We had to get out of that camper or we'd be mouse roasts for sure!

At last, we made it to the door and **BURST** outside.

We were just in time!

The **CRUELCAT EXPRESS** took off at breakneck speed!

I was so exhausted. I collapsed on the ground. **Big mistake!** Seconds later, a super-fit mouse on a bicycle built for three skidded to a stop inches from my snout. Can you guess who it was? It was Champ Strongpaws, of course!

"Hop on!" he squeaked. "We've got to **STOP** those cats!"

We jumped on the bike, and the three of us began to pedal **frantically**.

Sweat sprang from my fur. Did I mention I'm not much of a sportsmouse?

We had almost reached the camper . . .

We had almost reached the camper when we saw something **BLACK** and **SHINY** in the water. Was it a shark? Was it the **Loch Ness Mousester**?

No, it was a **black submarine** with the same inscription as the black camper: Cruelcat Express.

A large door opened on the sub.

Then the camper disappeared inside.

P.P. let out an **EVIL LAUGH** as the submarine took off into the night.

I was glad I had my camera on me. A cat with a *STEEL PAW* riding on a submarine?

YOU HAD TO SEE IT TO BELIEVE IT!

"LET'S GO!"

Soon the submarine sank into the churning waves and disappeared from sight. I stared out over the dark ocean, deep in thought. Even though the cats had gone, I was still worried. I wondered if and when P.P. would come back. I wondered what evil plans he was cooking up on Cat Island. I wondered if he was cooking up mice.

Suddenly, I began to feel sick to my stomach. Maybe it was the cycling. Maybe it was the stinky fish oil in my fur. But whatever it was, there was one thing I knew for sure. It was time to go home.

"Let's go!" I told my friends.

We rode back through the streets of New Mouse City.

At that moment, I saw some newspapers **fluttering** by in the breeze.

I had a brilliant idea. If I hurried, I could publish a **SPECIAL EDITION** of *The Rodent's Gazette.* It would be fabumouse!

SPECIAL EDITION

STOP THE PRESSES!

My friends dropped me off at *The Rodent's Gazette.*

I ran straight into the office.

"**Stop the presses!**" I squeaked at the top of my lungs. "We're going to do a **SPECIAL EDITION** of the *Gazette*. It's sensational news!"

I raced toward the pressroom with my staff following me down the hallway. My secretary, Mousella MacMouser, took notes as I explained my exciting adventure.

I told everyone about **Pussycat Pulverizer**'s plot to sell thousands of stolen CDs. I told them about his black camper and submarine, the Cruelcat Express, and about his whiny cousin Cleveland.

Then I showed everyone the **PHOTOS** I had taken.

I couldn't take my eyes off one shot of P.P. racing for the submarine. I felt like he was **STARING** right at me!

Cheese niblets! I was glad we had escaped from such an **EVIL** cat!

Stop the presses! **SPECIAL EDITION!**

Here are the photos I shot during that incredible adventure. I printed them in my newspaper.

The Cruelcat Express Submarine

Photo No. 1

Pussycat Pulverizer entering the Submarine

Photo No. 2

The Submarine going underwater

Photo No. 3

GET BACK TO WORK!

The special edition was a **big success**. I was so happy. I even got a note from my impossibly **HARD-TO-PLEASE** grandfather William Shortpaws.

It read:

Nice going, Geronimo!
Now get back to work!
Grandfather William

I smiled. My grandfather William was one **TOUGH** mouse. You might even say he was as tough as a cat!

BANANA BONANZA BUFFET

The next night, Hercule had a party at his house. He invited Champ, me, and all of my friends from *The Rodent's Gazette*.

I put on my best jacket. I combed my fur until it **gleamed**. Then I added a spritz of cologne. I felt **GREAT**.

I arrived at Hercule's house right on time. But when I rang the bell, disaster struck. First globs of **honey** rained down on my head. Then a fan blew a **cloud** of feathers at me. I looked like a mouse who had

A fan blew a cloud of feathers at me!

been attacked by a gang of crazed chickens!

I **STOMPED** into Hercule's kitchen, showering the place with feathers. Oh, how did I get myself into such a mess?

At that moment, I noticed a STRANGE scent in the air.

"Uh, what did you make for dinner, Hercule?" I asked suspiciously.

Hercule grinned. "You're not going to believe this, Stilton.

"Tonight I have whipped up what I like

to call a **Banana Bonanza Buffet**!" he squeaked. "I made **banana** appetizers, **banana** soup, **banana** cheese loaf, and even **banana** ice cream for dessert!"

I clutched my stomach. Did I mention I **hate** bananas?

I was feeling worse than ever. My tail had stuck to the countertop. There was a feather in my nose. And I was starving.

In the other room, I could hear Hercule

greeting our friends. Everyone was laughing and talking as the house filled with guests.

I listened for a minute and then I made a decision.

I found a piece of stale bread and a **crust of blue cheese** in Hercule's refrigerator. Then I took a shower, put on one of Hercule's robes, and joined my friends.

After all, it's not the food that makes a perfect dinner party — it's the company of good friends!

Here are some jokes we heard at Hercule's dinner party.

"I was walking under a window when a radio fell on my head," Nibbles tells his friend.

"Holey cheese! Did you get hurt?" asks his friend.

"No. Luckily, it was playing soft music!"

Furbrain and his wife leave for vacation.

At the airport, Furbrain stamps his paw and says,

"I should have brought the piano!"

"What for?" asks his wife.

"Because I left the plane tickets on it!"

Mrs. Rat is singing loudly in the shower.

"What did you do with the money?" asks Mr. Rat.

"What money?" replies Mrs. Rat.

"The money I gave you for singing lessons!"

RAT-MUNCHING RATTLESNAKES!

The following month, I was working quietly when I heard a **COMMOTION** outside my office.

A second later, my door burst open and Champ Strongpaws zoomed in. He was riding a bicycle built for two, which is also known as a **tandem bicycle**.

Before I could ask him why he was riding a bike with two seats, Champ rolled over my **tail** and skidded to a stop.

"Rat-munching rattlesnakes!" I screeched, jumping to my paws.

Champ grinned. "Mr. G, you must be reading my mind!" he squeaked. "I was just thinking about snakes. In fact, I came here to tell you about the exciting trip I have planned for us. Just imagine: a dry desert under the BLAZING sun, sand dunes as **far** as the eye can see, and **strange** wild animals like POISONOUS snakes and spiders as **large** as *chickens*!"

I shivered. What was Champ talking about? A trip? For the two of us? It was then that I noticed the SLEEPING BAGS, TENTS, AND CANTEENS attached to Champ's bicycle.

Oh, no! Not one of Champ's crazy bike races! I wasn't an athlete. Plus, I was way too busy at work.

In a daze, I listened as Champ went on about ALL OF THE THINGS WE WOULD DO AND SEE. We would pedal for miles on end, drinking **CACTUS** juice and frying eggs by the **HEAT** of the **blistering sun**.

Whew! I felt tired just imagining it. Without thinking, I plopped down on the back of Champ's bicycle.

I heard a triumphant screech.

"**YEAAAAAAAAAAAAAAAAAAAAAAAHHHHHHHH!**" Champ squeaked.

Then he began to pedal like a mad mouse.

"I knew you wouldn't miss this trip, Mr. G!" he cried. "*Adventure, here we come!*"

At first, I tried to stop him. Then I gave up and started to pedal.

Having a **wild** desert adventure might be sort of fun, after all. I mean, if a mouse like me could become a *singing sensation*, then I guess

aNYtHiNg ReaLLy iS PoSSibLe!

Want to read my next adventure?
I can't wait to tell you all about it!

THE KARATE MOUSE

Moldy mozzarella! When my friend Bruce
Hyena and his super-sporty cousin, Shorty
Tao, entered me in the Karate World
Championship, I couldn't believe it. I
wasn't in shape, and I didn't know a single
karate move. Plus, I only had one week
to train! How on earth was I going to
become a champion karate mouse in just
seven days?

And don't miss any of my other fabumouse adventures!

#1 LOST TREASURE OF THE EMERALD EYE

#2 THE CURSE OF THE CHEESE PYRAMID

#3 CAT AND MOUSE IN A HAUNTED HOUSE

#4 I'M TOO FOND OF MY FUR!

#5 FOUR MICE DEEP IN THE JUNGLE

#6 PAWS OFF, CHEDDARFACE!

#7 RED PIZZAS FOR A BLUE COUNT

#8 ATTACK OF THE BANDIT CATS

#9 A FABUMOUSE VACATION FOR GERONIMO

#10 ALL BECAUSE OF A CUP OF COFFEE

11 IT'S HALLOWEEN, YOU 'FRAIDY MOUSE!

#12 MERRY CHRISTMAS, GERONIMO!

#13 THE PHANTOM OF THE SUBWAY

#14 THE TEMPLE OF THE RUBY OF FIRE

#15 THE MONA MOUSA CODE

#16 A CHEESE-COLORED CAMPER

#17 WATCH YOUR WHISKERS, STILTON!

#18 SHIPWRECK ON THE PIRATE ISLANDS

#19 MY NAME IS STILTON, GERONIMO STILTON

#20 SURF'S UP, GERONIMO!

#21 THE WILD, WILD WEST

#22 THE SECRET OF CACKLEFUR CASTLE

A CHRISTMAS TALE

#23 VALENTINE'S DAY DISASTER

#24 FIELD TRIP TO NIAGARA FALLS

#25 THE SEARCH FOR SUNKEN TREASURE

#26 THE MUMMY WITH NO NAME

#27 THE CHRISTMAS TOY FACTORY

#28 WEDDING CRASHER

#29 DOWN AND OUT DOWN UNDER

#30 THE MOUSE ISLAND MARATHON

#31 THE MYSTERIOUS CHEESE THIEF

CHRISTMAS CATASTROPHE

#32 VALLEY OF THE GIANT SKELETONS

#33 GERONIMO AND THE GOLD MEDAL MYSTERY

#34 GERONIMO STILTON, SECRET AGENT

#35 A VERY MERRY CHRISTMAS

#36 GERONIMO'S VALENTINE

#37 THE RACE ACROSS AMERICA

#38 A FABUMOUSE SCHOOL ADVENTURE

#39 SINGING SENSATION

And don't forget to look for

#40 THE KARATE MOUSE

If you like my brother's adventures, be sure to read my books, too!

THEA STILTON AND THE DRAGON'S CODE

I couldn't believe it when I, Thea Stilton, was invited to teach a journalism class at Mouse Island's most prestigious university! I had no idea that once I arrived, I would meet five amazing students. What's more, I didn't realize that another student would disappear—and the rest of us would have to help solve the mystery! Holey Swiss cheese, it was an incredible adventure!

THEA STILTON AND THE MOUNTAIN OF FIRE

The Thea Sisters head to Australia to help solve a mystery on Nicky's family's small farm. It turns out that a flock of sheep is losing all its wool. The friends set off on a tour of Australia to search for a cure to the sheep's ailment. Of course, there are tons of obstacles in their way, and the mouselings must first climb over mountains, survive a flood, and avoid the traps of an invisible enemy! It's an adventure Down Under that they're sure to remember forever!

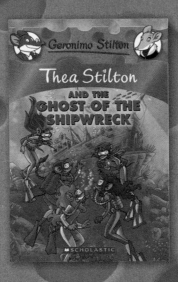

THEA STILTON AND THE GHOST OF THE SHIPWRECK

During a marine biology lesson at Mouseford Academy, the Thea Sisters learn about a mysterious shipwreck near Whale Island's Cormorant Rocks. According to legend, the ship was transporting a rare large diamond called Jasmine's Heart when it sank. When the biology teacher disappears, the mouselings search his laboratory for clues. The clues all point to the sunken shipwreck, and the only solution for the five mice is to dive into the deep ocean to solve the mystery.

Listen to a Double Dose of Geronimo's "Fabumouse" Adventures on Audio!

MORE 2-AUDIOBOOK PACKS AVAILABLE NOW:

ABOUT THE AUTHOR

 Born in New Mouse City, Mouse Island, Geronimo Stilton is Rattus Emeritus of Mousomorphic Literature and of Neo-Ratonic Comparative Philosophy. For the past twenty years, he has been running *The Rodent's Gazette,* New Mouse City's most widely read daily newspaper.

Stilton was awarded the Ratitzer Prize for his scoops on *The Curse of the Cheese Pyramid* and *The Search for Sunken Treasure.* He has also received the Andersen 2000 Prize for Personality of the Year. One of his bestsellers won the 2002 eBook Award for world's best ratlings' electronic book. His works have been published all over the globe.

In his spare time, Mr. Stilton collects antique cheese rinds and plays golf. But what he most enjoys is telling stories to his nephew Benjamin.

THE RODENT'S GAZETTE

1. Main entrance
2. Printing presses (where the books and newspaper are printed)
3. Accounts department
4. Editorial room (where the editors, illustrators, and designers work)
5. Geronimo Stilton's office
6. Storage space for Geronimo's books

Map of New Mouse City

1. Industrial Zone
2. Cheese Factories
3. Angorat International Airport
4. WRAT Radio and Television Station
5. Cheese Market
6. Fish Market
7. Town Hall
8. Snotnose Castle
9. The Seven Hills of Mouse Island
10. Mouse Central Station
11. Trade Center
12. Movie Theater
13. Gym
14. Catnegie Hall
15. Singing Stone Plaza
16. The Gouda Theater
17. Grand Hotel
18. Mouse General Hospital
19. Botanical Gardens
20. Cheap Junk for Less (Trap's store)
21. Parking Lot
22. Mouseum of Modern Art
23. University and Library
24. *The Daily Rat*
25. *The Rodent's Gazette*
26. Trap's House
27. Fashion District
28. The Mouse House Restaurant
29. Environmental Protection Center
30. Harbor Office
31. Mousidon Square Garden
32. Golf Course
33. Swimming Pool
34. Blushing Meadow Tennis Courts
35. Curlyfur Island Amusement Park
36. Geronimo's House
37. New Mouse City Historic District
38. Public Library
39. Shipyard
40. Thea's House
41. New Mouse Harbor
42. Luna Lighthouse
43. The Statue of Liberty

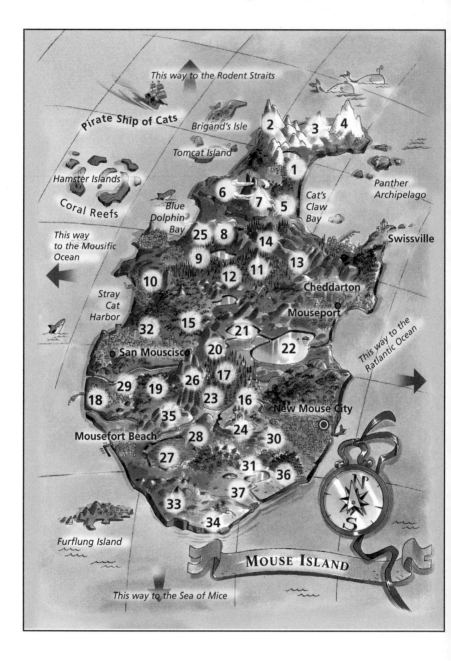

Map of Mouse Island

1. Big Ice Lake
2. Frozen Fur Peak
3. Slipperyslopes Glacier
4. Coldcreeps Peak
5. Ratzikistan
6. Transratania
7. Mount Vamp
8. Roastedrat Volcano
9. Brimstone Lake
10. Poopedcat Pass
11. Stinko Peak
12. Dark Forest
13. Vain Vampires Valley
14. Goose Bumps Gorge
15. The Shadow Line Pass
16. Penny Pincher Castle
17. Nature Reserve Park
18. Las Ratayas Marinas
19. Fossil Forest
20. Lake Lake
21. Lake Lakelake
22. Lake Lakelakelake
23. Cheddar Crag
24. Cannycat Castle
25. Valley of the Giant Sequoia
26. Cheddar Springs
27. Sulfurous Swamp
28. Old Reliable Geyser
29. Vole Vale
30. Ravingrat Ravine
31. Gnat Marshes
32. Munster Highlands
33. Mousehara Desert
34. Oasis of the Sweaty Camel
35. Cabbagehead Hill
36. Rattytrap Jungle
37. Rio Mosquito

Dear mouse friends,
Thanks for reading, and farewell
till the next book.
It'll be another whisker-licking-good
adventure, and that's a promise!

Geronimo Stilton